I0586182

FAITH

A SPIRITUAL FICTION SERIES

WALDMEER SERIES
BOOK 4

DONNA GODDARD

Second Edition 2023

Published by Donna Goddard

Victoria, Australia

Paperback ISBN: 978-0645729634

Large Print ISBN: 978-0645875560

Cover design by Donna Goddard

www.donnagoddard.com

CONTENTS

FOR NOTHING, FOR ALL

PART I
SUMMER

LOOK AFTER MY BOY

CHAPTER 1
A NEW YEAR

S pring had come and gone in Waldmeer, and it was well into summer. As Waldmeer is in the Southern Hemisphere, summer carries with it a new year.

Gabriel and Aristotle were travelling in the car to Waldmeer from Gabriel's apartment in Darnall. It was Aristotle's idea. Gabriel didn't like going to Waldmeer anymore.

Since Amira had mysteriously disappeared in early spring and her nasty cousin, Eve, had taken over the house, the whole of Waldmeer felt different. It was as if a light had gone out, and a dark cloud had spread over the town. Nevertheless, Aristotle wanted to visit, so Gabriel said yes. Gabriel said yes to almost everything Aristotle wanted.

They had been inseparable buddies for the last three months, even though Aristotle was only twelve and Gabriel was forty. He was an exceptional child—intelligent, kind, quick-witted, and delightful to be around. When Gabriel looked at Aristotle, a thought often popped into his mind, *Look after my boy.* He could not remember that they were Lady Faith's parting words when he and Aristotle entered the frame, which transported them from Borderfirma to Waldmeer.

"Tell me again why you want to visit Waldmeer," said Gabriel.

"I want to go and see my Aunt Eve's house," said Aristotle.

"I don't want to say anything mean, but do you realise that your Aunt Eve is not a particularly nice person?" said Gabriel. "She's not like you."

He wondered how two such different people could be so closely related. For that matter, Amira was also related to Eve, and that was an equally unfortunate genetic mismatch.

"Oh, I know that," said Aristotle. "Aunt Eve's much meaner than you would even care to know about."

"Then why do you want to go there?" asked Gabriel. "The house looks completely different from when your Aunt Amira had it."

The curtains were always drawn. The garden was overgrown with weeds, and the flowers didn't grow anymore. Gabriel thought about how Amira would sometimes say that one would have to try hard to have an ugly garden in Waldmeer because the rain, sunshine, and rich forest soil made everything grow without help.

"I have a feeling my mother might be back soon," said Aristotle.

"Do you?" asked Gabriel. "How do you know?"

"I dreamt it," said Aristotle.

"Oh," said Gabriel tolerantly.

Aristotle was always dreaming of weird and wonderful things. Gabriel had become acclimatised to Amira's dreaming habits, so he took it in his stride.

After a few minutes, he said, "I know you miss your mother, but she may be some time yet."

He felt that there was a real chance that Aristotle's mother (whoever and wherever she was) might never return.

After all, he thought, *what sort of mother would leave their child with Eve?*

When Gabriel returned to Earth from Borderfirma with Aristotle in tow, he was very disoriented. He told Aristotle that he felt unwell and that something was mentally wrong with him. He could not assimilate the memory of Borderfirma with the reality of his life on Earth.

That first evening in Darnall, Aristotle contacted his mother telepathically. Lady Faith did not remember Borderfirma when she was on Earth as Amira. However, for his safety, Aristotle had retained his Borderfirma memory. He asked his mother how to help Gabriel. She told him to whisper the following words into Gabriel's ear and that the Great Ones would make sure that it entered his mind as an uncontested reality.

Aristotle crept into Gabriel's room. He crouched next to him as he was deeply sleeping.

"When you wake up," said Aristotle quietly and clearly, "you will not remember Borderfirma. Your only recollection of Amira will be the Amira you know on Earth. You will not be able to recall her as Lady Faith, ruler of the Borderfirma Mountains, mother of Bethany, Malik, and me, and grandmother of Lentilly. You will believe that I am the child of Eve's sister, one of Amira's cousins. You will also believe Amira sent me to you while my mother was away, so I do not have to live with my Aunt Eve."

Aristotle repeated this several times until he felt that Gabriel had absorbed it into his subconscious mind. On waking, Gabriel told Aristotle that he had slept like a baby and felt marvellous.

While driving along the peaceful country road, Gabriel asked, "What's your mother's name?"

"Faith," said Aristotle. "Her name is Faith."

"That's a nice name," said Gabriel.

Hopefully, Faith and Eve are like chalk and cheese, day and night, he thought.

"My mother is nothing like Aunt Eve," said Aristotle, reading Gabriel's thoughts. "She is a true queen."

"Yes," said Gabriel. "I'm sure she is."

Many a twelve-year-old boy thinks that his mother is a queen, thought Gabriel.

He remembered how Amira had once told him that the family romance must eventually be outgrown. He recalled many things that Amira had told him over the years. He wished that she would come back. Or, at least, he hoped she was alright wherever she was.

It's strange, he thought, *how some people's words stay inside us and have the power to change us, and other people's words are powerless, no matter how intelligent they may sound.*

"How old is your mother?" asked Gabriel.

"I believe she is fifty now," said Aristotle.

CHAPTER 2
CRYSTAL BALL

I n the *Borderfirma Mountains:*

Ten years had passed in Borderfirma. Time there is not like Earth time. It is not necessarily faster. Sometimes, it is slower. But not always. It is just different.

Lady Faith was fifty, Bethany was thirty, Malik was twenty-four, and baby Lentil was, believe it or not, ten. For the past ten years, Lady Faith and her mother had been training Bethany to take over the running of the Borderfirma Mountains. Malik was now one of Odin's most valued warriors in the Great Valley. And Lentilly had been busy playing with life and growing up.

Lady Faith had been away many times to the other dimensions. However, she had never been able to return to Earth because she had given that ability to her sister, Lady Evanora (Eve on Earth), in exchange for Aristotle's freedom.

A few days ago, while on an inter-dimensional trip, Lady Faith was told that Lady Evanora had returned from Earth to her kingdom, the Borderfirma Lowlands. Evanora had not anticipated Earth's primitive energetic consistency. It was much heavier than what she was used to in Borderfirma. It did not significantly affect Lady Faith because she prepared herself before her trips. Eve, however, found that it made her feel lethargic and depressed. Many of her supernatural abilities lost their potency. In disgust, she returned to her Borderfirma home, announcing to her subjects that Earth was entirely overrated and that one would be a fool ever to want to go there.

Although Lady Faith was thrilled to know that Eve was out of Waldmeer and away from its residents, she also knew that she still couldn't regain her ability to travel there in human form, as she had legitimately handed that over to Evanora. To her surprise, Lady Faith was told that she would be returning to Earth again soon. She was further told,

> You cannot now or in the future return to Earth as Amira. You will return as Faith—mother of Bethany, Malik, and Aristotle, Eve's sister, and Amira's cousin. You will be taking Bethany, Malik, and Lentilly with you.

Lady Faith immediately recalled visiting Nina and Odin in the Great Valley a few years ago. In the evening, Nina told Bethany that she would do a reading for her from her crystal ball. Bethany was very excited and entered the forbidden territory of Nina's bedroom. It looked like the bedroom of any old aunt with a religious bent. There was a large picture on the wall of an angel protecting two small children walking in trepidation on a rickety bridge. There were many religious statues from numerous traditions—Jesus and Mary, Buddha and Kwan Yin, Brahma, Vishnu, and Shiva. There were also pictures of Islamic geometric patterns and Arabic calligraphy. There was a single bed somewhere under a pile of clothes.

Nina ceremoniously opened her wardrobe, which was stuffed to overflow with God only knows what. She solemnly pulled out a large, clear crystal ball and carefully placed it in the middle of the small table. Then, all was utterly still, and time stopped.

Bethany's eyes were fixed on the heavy, mesmerising glass ball. She could see the red velvet underneath it. There were many lights inside it. She couldn't tell if they were reflections from the room or came from somewhere else.

What is it saying? she wondered. *What does it see?*

She dared not break the sacred atmosphere by asking.

Suddenly, Nina broke the spell in the room, stood up, covered the ball with a cloth and said, "Well, that's that."

"What's that?" said Bethany. "What did it say?"

"It said you will meet your future husband on Earth," said Nina.

"Earth? On Earth? Oh, how wonderful," cooed Bethany. "I've always wanted to go there. But how?"

"I don't know," said Nina. "Why are you asking me? I don't know anything."

"But what about the Borderfirma Mountains?" said Bethany. "I can't leave."

"I don't know," repeated Nina.

"How will I get to Earth?" asked Bethany again. "I don't have my mother's ability to travel inter-dimensionally. And how will I find my husband?"

Nina shuffled Bethany back out into the lounge room and refused to answer any more of her questions.

CHAPTER 3
SALT AND PEPPER

Back in Waldmeer:

Back in Waldmeer: As they got to the bottom of Amira's hill, Gabriel looked with concern at Aristotle and said, "I told you not to get excited."

He worried that Aristotle's boyish innocence would lead to disappointment. To Gabriel's astonishment, Amira's old house looked completely different.

Aristotle gave a whoop of joy, jumped out of the car while it was still moving, and ran to the people in the front garden. It most certainly wasn't Eve. Nor was it Amira. It was a woman Gabriel had never seen before, a couple of younger adults, and a girl of around ten.

Aristotle ran to the group and practically bowled the woman over. The young man, in his early twenties, was huge. He lifted Aristotle as if he were a feather.

"Wow!" said Aristotle, "Look at you, Malik. You are the biggest person I've ever seen. You are even bigger than Odin."

"Not quite," laughed Malik.

"And Bethany," said Aristotle, "You are... a lady. You look like Mother."

Turning to Lentilly, he said, "This can't be baby Lentil."

"I'm no baby," said Lentilly with the dignity of a princess. "And my name is Lentilly, not Lentil."

Making her case clear, she relaxed and threw her arms around Aristotle.

"We are almost the same age," she said. "I'm not on my own anymore."

"She has been talking nonstop about having a brother ever since we knew we were coming," said Bethany.

"I'm your uncle," said Aristotle with a smile, "not your brother. So, treat me with respect."

"No hope of that, matey," said Malik, putting a protective arm around Aristotle.

Gabriel was standing nearby, watching them, totally absorbed in their family reunion. He suddenly realised that he probably shouldn't be standing there staring. The woman walked to him with an outstretched hand.

"You must be Gabriel," said Faith, shaking his hand warmly.

Gabriel stared at her and thought, *My God. She looks exactly like Amira, but older.*

"Amira has told me so much about you," continued Faith. "I feel I know you already."

Gabriel shuffled and wondered what Amira would have told her.

"How can I ever thank you for having my son for these last three months?" said Faith. "I know Amira sent him to you so he wouldn't have to stay with his Aunt Eve. I'm so sorry about my sister, Eve. She is a problem. We don't know what to do about her, but she has gone now, and the children and I have the house."

"Amira is not coming back then?" said Gabriel with sad eyes.

Faith hesitated, but it had to be said. "I'm so sorry. She is not coming back."

Gabriel looked away. The small group eyed each other with apprehension. No one knew what to say.

"Oh, well, that's life, isn't it?" said Gabriel, trying to smile.

Aristotle walked towards Gabriel and said softly, "Don't worry. You have all of us."

Gabriel looked a bit embarrassed and went to leave. He heard a loud bird call and saw, in the nearby forest, a family grouping of wedge-tailed eagles. He thought they must be the birds he had seen some months ago from the bungalow.

"We call the Dad, Aquilla," said Faith as her eyes trailed Gabriel's into the tree tops.

She pointed back to the garden and said, "I've pulled out some of the biggest weeds and given it a good watering."

Gabriel looked at Faith as she walked over to a pile of weeds to dump another lot. She had short, uncoloured, salt-and-pepper hair. Her face had no makeup, and she wore blue shorts and a plain cream T-shirt. Everything about her looked simple and... something else. He couldn't put his finger on it. There was nothing about her that was offensive and nothing about her that was attention-seeking. It was as if her body functioned so well and silently that she barely noticed it, except that she needed it. A thought passed through his mind.

It is not the frame that matters, but the picture. Make sure that the picture is beautiful. The frame is only there to draw the eyes to the picture.

He didn't know where the thought came from, but it seemed somehow appropriate. It was what Zufar (Bethany, Malik, and Aristotle's father) had written on the frame that had transported Aristotle and Gabriel from the Borderfirma Mountains to Waldmeer.

That whole family has something mysterious about them, thought Gabriel. *Maybe, weird. Maybe, wonderful. Either way, they are not normal.*

"I'll call you in a few days," Aristotle called to Gabriel as he headed for the cottage's front door.

"Thank you for looking after my boy," said Faith with calm, steady eyes.

Gabriel knew that she was referring to Aristotle, but the tone of her voice (or was it the look in her eyes) suggested that she may not have been referring exclusively to Aristotle.

A DIFFERENT APPROACH

CHAPTER 4
WARLORD

After two days in Waldmeer, Malik said to his mother, "Enough lounging around. Today, I will get a job."

"Alright," said Faith hesitantly. "Do you have a particular sort of job in mind?"

Malik had spent the first fourteen years of his life in a palace and the next ten in the Great Valley. He wasn't overly qualified for Earth work. Aristotle, who was standing nearby, smiled. He had been on Earth long enough to realise the problem with Malik getting a job.

"I have many abilities," said Malik. "Someone will want me."

Deciding not to dampen his enthusiasm, Faith refrained from advising him about how things worked in Waldmeer, but instead said, "Good luck. Anyone who gets you will be lucky."

Malik looked like he agreed and went out the door like a warrior going into an unknown battle. He walked up and down the main street, perusing businesses and reading notices. He then cased the side streets. He stopped at Vibes, the yoga studio, and his eyes were drawn to the open door. Sri, the studio's owner, waved to him. Malik nodded back.

"Good morning," said Salt on his way into his healing room.

"Good morning, Sir," said Malik.

Vibes was the closest thing to Malik's energetic disposition, but somehow, it didn't feel right. We are not necessarily called to the place most resonant with our vibration. Malik glanced across the street. He saw a rundown gym called Waldmeer Warriors. Crossing the road, he surveyed the gym through the dirty window. It was a dump. He rolled his eyes at the sort of *warriors* who would train there. Nevertheless, something pulled him inside.

There was a man on the front desk gazing at the television. He didn't bother to stop watching. Malik strode over to the free weights. The heaviest dumbbells were dusty from lack of use. The lighter ones were strewn all over the room untidily. He wondered if there were enough plates to stack onto the bar for a squat. A skinny kid, around sixteen, was watching him in the corner. Once seen, the kid abruptly returned to his bicep curls.

Boys that age think that being big is all about arms, thought Malik.

He went to the desk and said, "I'd like to speak to the boss."

"I'm the boss," said the man. "What do you want?"

If you are the boss, no wonder this place is in the state it is in, thought Malik.

"I'm interested in applying for a job as a personal trainer."

"What are your qualifications?" asked the man.

"I don't have formal qualifications," replied Malik, "but I have had rigorous training in the mountains."

The man momentarily looked at Malik.

"Yeah, right," he said. "Our personal trainers are highly qualified. Come back when you have a qualification."

He went back to the television.

Malik walked over to the wall and studied the notices of the supposedly highly trained personal trainers.

Pathetic, he thought.

He turned his eyes to the boy.

"What's your name, boy?" asked Malik.

"Michael," said the boy so softly that he had to repeat it several times before Malik could hear him.

"Why are you here?" asked Malik.

The boy squirmed and said, "Ah, you know. To get big. 'Cause of the other guys and all."

Malik picked up two smaller dumbbells and handed them to the boy.

"You are going too heavy," he said. "And bad form. Halve the weight. Double the reps. Contract your bicep as you curl."

"And do some work on your triceps," he added while striding away. "They are three-quarters of your upper arm."

Deciding on a different approach, Malik politely said to the boss, "What about if you give me a trial? I'll get a certificate, and, in the meantime, I'll find all my own clients. You have nothing to lose."

The man hesitated and was about to decline when Malik said, "I already have a client."

The boss raised his eyebrows in interest.

Malik walked over to the boy and said loudly, "I am

training Michael. He is interested in the bodybuilding competition that you have up there on the wall."

Malik pointed to the poster that said, *Annual Darnall Junior Bodybuilding Competition*. Michael stood there dumbly but didn't say it wasn't true.

"Okay," said the man. "You're on trial."

When they were alone, the boy mumbled something to Malik about having no money.

"Don't worry, kid," said Malik. "I'll train you for free while I get my certificate. Then, when we are both on our feet, I will charge you a lot. So, prepare to be a success. See you, same time, tomorrow morning."

The boy walked out of the gym three inches taller.

By the end of the month, Malik had already been nick-named the Warlord—the Warlord of the Waldmeer Warriors.

CHAPTER 5
PIXIE

F aith and Aristotle were on the bus to Darnall. Aristotle was spending the afternoon with Gabriel, and Faith was going to the shops.

~

GABRIEL HAD BEEN to Waldmeer a few times at Aristotle's request and became more familiar with the family. Faith had been reserved when Gabriel visited, not because she didn't want to connect with him, but because the possibility had not gone unrecognised that he could be the husband that Bethany was supposed to find on Earth.

Faith felt that if she kept in the background, after a while, it would become clear if there was any interest between Gabriel and Bethany. There wasn't. The thought didn't even cross Gabriel's mind.

As for Bethany, she was an intelligent young woman. She probably would have considered Gabriel if there had been an obvious interest from him. However, she was mature enough to know that trying to get someone interested in us (who is not) is a painful and pointless endeavour. There are many people in the world. Some are for us. Most are not.

After being satisfied that she could see no swirling energetic pull between Gabriel and Bethany, another thought popped into Faith's mind. She looked at Malik. Then at Gabriel. Malik and Gabriel?

Telling herself that we can turn ourselves into a mental minefield if we follow the trail of all our thoughts, she shook her head and brushed the thought aside.

Faith walked with Aristotle to Gabriel's apartment in Darnall and continued across the bridge to the Darnall shops. She had decided to modify her approach to Gabriel. Not only did he have no interest in Bethany (or Malik), but he also appeared to have little interest in her. She stopped at Mirko Merven's Hair Salon and read a poster advertising,

Makeover in the Middle
with Merven the Magician.

Mirko eyed her up and down and came towards her with a smile.

"May I help you?" he asked as if it were a rhetorical question.

Faith pointed to the poster and said, "I'm thinking of a cut and colour?"

"Yes, of course, dear," said Mirko. "When?"

"I don't suppose you could do it now?" asked Faith.

"I have a cancellation, so you are in luck," said Mirko.

After being seated and given peppermint tea and a consultation, Mirko and his assistant agreed that a soft blonde-brown and pixie cut would be best.

"Have you ever coloured your hair?" asked Mirko.

"Not for the last ten years," answered Faith.

"Hmm..." said Mirko. "Your hair is already short, but we will give it a bit of an edge so it looks like a style."

"I must admit that I normally cut it myself," Faith said apologetically.

Mirko coughed and said, "Pixie cut will look much better than a do-it-yourself job."

When out of earshot, he said to his assistant, "I think she has been living with the pixies if she thinks she can get away with uncoloured, self-cut hair."

He then added more kindly, although still condescendingly, "Come on. Let's fix her up."

When Faith went to get Aristotle, Gabriel said, "Wow, that looks great."

Then he immediately turned his attention to another topic.

Faith gazed out the window at the green paddocks and grazing cows on the return bus trip.

I thought that Gabriel would see who I am, she mused.

In the Borderfirma Mountains, people see internally, not externally. Others are recognised by their energy field, not by their appearance or personality.

Gabriel can't see me, thought Amira. *To him, I'm a different person. I probably am a somewhat different person after having spent ten years away.*

Aristotle pointed to the distant sea.

I can't make him interested in me, thought Amira. *I didn't make him interested in Amira so many years ago. Nor can I arrange it now.*

"Look, Mum, between the hills," said Aristotle. "There is Waldmeer. We are almost home."

WITCHES OF WURT
WURT KOORT

CHAPTER 6
WITCHES RULE

On the way to Darnall:

The bus driver announced that there would be a half-hour stop at Wurt Wurt Koort to change a tyre. The road from Waldmeer to Darnall ran through the hills of the Lelek Forest. At the highest point was the little town of Wurt Wurt Koort. From the Wurt Wurt Koort Town Hall, one could see inland to Darnall. In the other direction, one could make out the sea.

At one time, Wurt Wurt Koort was a thriving, respectable hill town. Thus, the presence of a somewhat pretentious town hall. However, the death of a local child changed all that, and now it was barely surviving. It was rumoured to be run by witches.

They weren't bad witches. Many had businesses and were visited, with some success, for healing, readings, and other mysterious-type activities. There was a leadership group or coven of thirteen. The women in the coven ranged from fifty to positively ancient. Their headquarters were the local cafe, the *Wurt Wurt Koort Tearooms*.

It was a brilliant morning, promising to be a hot day, although the air in the hills was always cooler than in Darnall. Faith loved watching the passing trees from the bus window. They were so majestic, yet so humble.

Her mind wandered to a year ago when Gabriel was living with her in Waldmeer after accepting a teaching position at Darnall College. It was a happy, contented time. She recalled a conversation they had one morning about dreaming. Gabriel had looked at her intently and said, "Well, you are awake now and here. Just remember that, or one day you will dream yourself to another place altogether."

Faith hadn't thought of that conversation for a long time.

From the mouths of babes, she thought. *I did dream myself to another place altogether. Maybe he wasn't such a baby after all.*

The bus pulled up next to the Wurt Wurt Koort Town Hall. Faith glanced at the road sign with graffiti saying, *Witches Rule*. It wasn't difficult to recognise the witches.

With more pleasure than anticipated, she walked past a large wooden table with about eight women in the tearooms. Not a coloured head in sight. Most had long hair. Some wore it loose. Some had braids. All were completely unfashionable and totally at home with it. Their clothes were a great outburst of colour, and long flowing skirts were the preferred dress code. Several loud and enthusiastic conversations were going on at once in the group. One woman had a grandchild in the highchair next to her.

Faith sat close enough to observe the women, but far enough away so that she could. Although they didn't skip a beat in their conversations, she knew that they were aware of her presence both physically and energetically. Yet, they said nothing nor looked in her direction. Looking is only for those who cannot see.

Usually intimidating to outsiders, especially when they were en masse, the witches were well aware of Faith's calm interest in them. There is an old saying that a thief knows another thief straight away. Likewise, do witches.

The bus tooted, and Faith reluctantly left.

Until we meet again, she thought.

Or were *they* thinking it?

CHAPTER 7
DELUSION DISSOLUTION

Faith was travelling to Darnall to introduce herself to Thomas and Grace. She had heard that Thomas was renovating the old Darnall Arcade. It attracted growing tourist interest due to its innovative design.

Thomas and Grace were in their shop, Mac & Mac. Both were delighted to meet Faith as Amira's cousin. They were too discreet to ask about Amira's absence, so they talked instead about Faith's similarity to Amira in looks and demeanour. Grace showed Faith the rest of the arcade, pointing out Teresa and Bryan's shop, Handspun. Like every other shop in the arcade, it was flourishing.

"Teresa and Bryan have just returned from their honeymoon," said Grace. "They had a lovely family wedding in the Waldmeer Convent."

"That's wonderful," said Faith.

"It's great for Teresa's girls," said Grace. "Bryan is a good stepdad."

"How old are Teresa's girls?" asked Faith.

"Josephine is sixteen, and Rebecca is fourteen," said Grace.

Growing up, thought Faith.

"Just between you and me," said Grace with only good-will, "I think it took Bryan a bit of convincing to get Teresa to marry again, but now she's totally on board."

"I hope so," laughed Faith. "Too late to abandon ship."

"And too early," smiled Grace.

Grace has grown—her confidence, sense of humour, and general happiness, thought Faith.

Only one of the original four healing shops remained in the arcade. The rest had closed or moved because the rent was too high or the new, vibrant feel of the arcade did not align with their business mentality.

"Thomas always says, 'What isn't growing is dying,'" said Grace.

"Have you met Faith yet, Gabriel?" asked Grace as he walked into the arcade.

"I certainly have," said Gabriel, kissing them both. "Amira asked me to look after Faith's son for a little while."

"It was more than a little while," Faith said apologetically.

Although Faith had told herself that Gabriel couldn't see who she was, it wasn't exactly true. He could see her. It would have been impossible for him not to know, at some level, that Faith was precisely the same as Amira.

He recognised her alright, but he didn't want to. He was hurt that the Amira he knew had gone away. More than that, he was angry about all the challenging things that came with Amira. It wasn't even a matter of whether she was right or not. He didn't want another person like Amira in his life.

And this version was older and would be even more *Amira* than Amira was.

Relationships always bring about the dissolution of our delusions. And thus, it would have remained except that all Life hears of such defeating self-talk is,

Blah, blah, blah. I see your lips movin', but I can't hear a thing.

Life always does what It wants.

CHAPTER 8
BLIGHT IN THE NIGHT

O n the return bus trip, a woman about Faith's age sat beside her. After nodding to her, Faith remained quiet. Unless a situation called for her to speak, she didn't. She had no need for idle conversation.

As the bus rattled through Wurt Wurt Koort, the woman said, "I was born in this town. Pity about it these days."

"Really?" said Faith.

"I'm not from the witch bloodline," laughed the woman.

"I see," said Faith, urging her on.

"When I was a child, there was a fight for leadership in the witch clan," said the woman. "Normally, we all lived side-by-side with no problems. There was a lot of respect in those days. However, the witch clan fight got nastier and nastier. Rumour had it that the head witch had become dark in her old age. There was a challenge for leadership from one of the younger witches. As the old witch worsened, she lost her supporters and was eventually told to leave. She left but scrawled on the town hall that night,

Hold onto your daughters,
try as you might.
They'll be gone by daylight,
carnage of our fight.

The witches cleaned up the graffiti, but everyone had seen it. A vindictive witch is no match for ordinary folk. For a while, no one did anything. We all waited. Three months passed, and then the ten-year-old daughter of the contesting witch died from a mysterious illness. That was it. If the new head witch couldn't keep her own daughter safe, how could she protect everyone else's daughters? Everyone left except the witches. Even some of them left."

CHAPTER 9
DANCING,
MAGICK, AND FUN

That evening, Faith told Bethany all about Wurt Wurt Koort. The conversation riveted Bethany, so Faith was not surprised when Bethany told her she would visit Wurt Wurt Koort.

"Leave Lentilly here with me," said Faith. "Have a lovely day."

Both knew she was saying, *Be careful.*

Bethany loved the place, but it wasn't only love. She saw a need and knew it was hers to fill.

A few days later, Bethany said, "I'm going to start a children's class at Wurt Wurt Koort. It will be all the things that come naturally to Borderfirma people. All things happy—dancing, music, and a little magic for interest's sake."

She had always been a creative soul.

"The thing missing from Wurt Wurt Koort is happiness," said Bethany. "It went when that child died. People know I am not from the witch bloodline, and they will see I am safe in Wurt Wurt Koort. They will trust that the little town is fine and venture back into it. They think I don't have magic because I'm not a witch."

Bethany and Faith laughed at that thought. The magic in Bethany was more than many of those witches combined.

The class was called *Dance, Magick, and Fun.* It went so well that, within the month, Bethany expanded her budding business and rented a cottage in Wurt Wurt Koort.

The two future queens of the Borderfirma Mountains, thought Faith, *on their own, in the domain of the witches.*

She went outside and listened to the waves at the bottom of her hill, so familiar and untroubled.

Like everyone else, thought Faith, *they must walk their own path. And they have to grow into their right to rule.*

She saw the eagle family at the edge of the forest. The babies were growing fast.

Anyway, the girls need to enjoy life, thought Faith. *Who knows what will come their way?*

Bethany and Lentilly lived in Wurt Wurt Koort with all their light and beauty, and the little town seemed to skip with joy and relief.

WURT WURT
KOORT TEAROOMS

CHAPTER 10
RYBERT'S QUOTES

F aith was meeting Bethany and Lentilly in the Wurt Wurt Koort Tearooms. It was the only shop doing well in the little town. That was because of Rybert. He was the owner, manager, and main staff member. He was also the son of a coven witch. That is why the witches met in the cafe. He understood them. He understood them, but he kept his distance. He loved them, but he loved most people. He treated everyone who came into the cafe as his friend. They responded in kind and wondered why they didn't stop more often when driving through.

Every customer got one of Rybert's quotes with their coffee. The quotes were a mixture of famous and witchy ones from books, movies, and his community. The witch quotes were everyone's favourites. Some were thought-provoking, but Rybert was mostly a comedian. He made fun of himself, his world, and everything else he thought he could get away with. One of his quotes was about witches working naked.

"The last thing I want to see is a naked witch!" he would say.

That was because the majority of the witches in Wurt Wurt Koort were his mother's age. Anyway, he wasn't overly interested in naked women. Although he was around forty, he wasn't married. It probably wouldn't have been to a woman if he had been, least of all to a witch.

As much as he was the first to criticise and make fun of the witches, Rybert was protective of them. They raised him and passed on more knowledge and abilities than he knew.

One of his little amusements was knowing what people would order before they told him. He usually kept that party trick for the children because adults find such things disconcerting.

Rybert sometimes said of the witches, "You gotta love 'em, but you better be sure to leave 'em."

He was a character. And thank God he was, as he kept Wurt Wurt Koort alive. Of course, he was well aware of Bethany and Lentilly's presence in town. He quickly made friends with them and saw them, most days, when they came in after their morning walk. He casually kept dropping advice to Bethany as he wanted her and her business to survive and thrive. He knew how much the town needed new blood.

"This is my mother," said Bethany to Rybert as she, Faith, and Lentilly sat in the corner of the tearooms.

"Oh, yes, hun," said Rybert, "we saw her before we saw you."

Turning to Faith, he said, "That morning when you came here when the Darnall bus stopped to change a tyre, we saw you then. We see everything here, pumpkin. I could tell by my mother and her witchy buds' reaction that they were interested in you, but we didn't know we would get your two sweethearts to keep."

CHAPTER 11
PERSONAL IDENTIFICATION

After getting off the return bus at Waldmeer, Faith went to the automatic teller machine. She intended to access Amira's bank account. However, as she had been in the Borderfirma Mountains for so long, she had trouble remembering her personal identification number. She tried numerous combinations unsuccessfully.

She could feel the person behind her watching. It didn't bother her, as she could tell the person's feeling was more amusement than anything else. Finally, accepting defeat, she turned around to apologise for keeping the other customer waiting so long.

"Oh!" said Faith.

"You're back," said Farkas. "Your hair looks good."

Farkas knew she was Amira. She wasn't sure what to do about that. Maybe nothing. He seemed to take her older appearance in his stride. It probably helped that he didn't see her much. The day-to-day physical elements of life become less important. Perhaps, less seeable.

"Try it again," said Farkas.

This time, the PIN worked.

Faith walked the long way home by the sea. The beach was busy with many summer tourists. Toddlers pranced in and out of the water, cavorting with the waves. Ignorant of the scale of what they were entering, the children became braver with each screaming attempt to meet the great mass of water on their own terms.

Tolerant of the children and their desires, the waves obliged until it was time to remind them of their insignificance. Without missing a beat, the current pushed them over like a tiny bit of seaweed in the infinite, life-giving ocean. After being rescued and consoled by their mothers, the game would begin again.

This is us, thought Faith. *We assign roles to everyone in an attempt to control them. The roles can be reasonable or preposterous. Either way, when we realise that others do not agree to the terms of the role we have assigned to them, we get upset. Is it their fault? Surely, they are simply following what they want for themselves.*

A mother called out from the shore, and one of the toddlers turned and laughed, before running back into the waves.

We mustn't invent roles for others in the hope it will make us happy, thought Faith. *Who are we to invent such things? Can the tiny seaweed tell the vast ocean what it must do?*

A gust of wind whipped past, and the seagulls erupted into loud, scrambling cries over something in the sand.

What wills to grow will grow, thought Faith, *and what wills to flow will flow.*

MIRROR OF LIFE

CHAPTER 12
LAND IN THE MIDDLE

*I*n the *Borderfirma Mountains:*

Ten years ago, in Borderfirma, when Bethany was told that she would begin training to take over the running of the Borderfirma Mountains, she asked where her mother would be going.

Lady Faith replied, "The Inner Circle is not the end of the journey. There is another land. It lies between Borderfirma and the higher dimensions. It is a place where all illusions are dismantled. Once there, the pull to higher dimensions is very great."

Seeing her daughter's concern, Lady Faith added, "Oh, don't worry. I'm not staying there. They told me I'd be back and that I would also be returning to Earth."

Indeed, Lady Faith returned to both. This is what happened some years ago in that mystical and marvellous place, the land in the middle of Borderfirma and the higher dimensions, Tierramedio.

CHAPTER 13
TIERRAMEDIO

*S*ome years ago, in Tierramedio:

Lady Faith woke in a place that she had never been before. She found herself walking down a long, empty corridor. At the end of the corridor was a door with a sign saying, *H & C Headquarters.*

Once through the door, she was pleased to see someone she knew sitting at the reception desk. It was Kathleen, Thomas's partner of several years, who had passed on.

"Kathleen!" said Faith. "How lovely to see you."

There seemed to be no need to explain whether she was Amira or Lady Faith.

"They told me you were coming," said Kathleen.

She looked about the same age as when she left Earth, but she didn't have any of the heaviness common to Earth people. She was light and serene.

"How is Thomas?" asked Kathleen.

"I haven't been to Earth, myself, for quite a while," said Faith. "However, the last time I was there (and I don't think much Earth time has passed since then), he had moved to

Darnall and was working on fixing up the old Darnall Arcade.

Kathleen looked at Faith enquiringly. She wanted more information about how he was really doing.

"He struggled after you left," said Faith.

Kathleen nodded and said, "There's no avoiding it. Pain that is. It is the way of Earth."

"What does *H & C Headquarters* stand for?" asked Faith.

Kathleen pointed to two doors on either side of her desk. One door had the word *Heal* above it. The other had the word *Create* above it.

"You are at the *Heal and Create Headquarters*," she said. "We are the portal to the land in the middle of Borderfirma and higher dimensions, Tierramedio."

"Do both doors lead to Tierramedio?" asked Faith.

"No," said Kathleen, "only one of them does."

Faith looked at the doors.

Creating is higher than healing, she thought. *It is primal. However, in order to create profoundly, we must first heal.*

"One door leads to Earth," said Kathleen.

"Oh, that makes it easy," said Faith. "The *Heal* door is Earth. I need to go back there. My friends are there, and I have things to do."

Faith wondered if this was how the Masters would get her back to Earth.

"The other door is the entrance to Tierramedio," said Kathleen. "Tierramedio is a centre of creation."

"Create what exactly?" asked Lady Faith.

"I'm not sure," said Kathleen. "I'm not allowed to go through the Tierramedio door. That is why I am here at reception. I don't want to return to Earth, but I am not yet ready for Tierramedio. I am happy here, and one day I will walk through that door."

There will be another way back to Earth, thought Faith. *I need to keep growing.*

She walked to the Create door.

"How do I open it?" asked Faith.

As she said the words, the door, the reception desk, and Kathleen vanished.

ON THE OTHER side of the door was a large, plain mirror. From the corner of her eye, Faith saw many faces that were constantly changing. If she looked at them directly, they disappeared. She instinctively knew that the faces were her own from numerous lifetimes, both on Earth and elsewhere.

Surprisingly, it wasn't particularly interesting. It was like a catalogue of books she had already read and did not wish to read again.

Something pulled her away from the mirror towards a spacious, blue room. It had nothing in it, but it felt alive and inviting. The room had a striking purity as if it had never been contaminated by anything unlike itself.

A man walked towards her. It was the Master from the Garden of Garourinn. Faith knew that this Master had only visited Earth once in human form. Once was enough. What he left behind was healing Earth, even now, thousands of years later.

Faith bowed her head. The Master accepted her salutation. Masters do not need recognition. They have no ego to accept such things, but we need to give it.

"You looked into the Mirror of Life," said the Master.

"Yes," said Faith. "Is that what the mirror is called?"

The Master did not answer her question but said, "You have come for something."

"Yes," said Faith.

She knew that she had come for something, but if he asked her what it was, she wouldn't be able to articulate an answer.

"If you want it," said the Master, "you must vanish."

Until this point, Faith felt quite wonderful in Tierramedio. Wonderful and expectant. Although she did not vanish as the Master suggested, the feeling of wonderfulness did.

A disturbing, distracting noise started yelling in her ear. Something was fighting inside her. The Master had released it. She stood still and could feel a storm of movement rising within. Every face she had seen in the Mirror of Life seemed to be screaming at her, *Danger*. As it did not subside, she had to move away from the Master to make it more bearable.

After a few minutes, Faith heard a little voice in the centre of the crazy ones, "What have you got to lose? What are you hanging onto?"

Was it the Master speaking? Was it her inner voice? Faith wasn't sure. She thought of all her lifetimes. She saw the countless miseries of all those she loved, all those she didn't know, and all those who weren't even born yet.

Again, the little voice spoke, "Trust. You have not come this far to turn back now. You are almost there. Have faith."

Faith? thought Faith.

Remembering her name, she suddenly said out loud, "Alright, I'm done."

There was a loud smash of glass breaking. It was the Mirror of Life. Then, everything went black. It was utterly silent.

Everything disappeared—the blue room, the Master, her body, her memories, her desires, her separation, and even herself. She dared not look to see what was left, but there seemed to be no one left to do the looking.

Slowly, the light came back, the blue room returned, and the Master stood there.

Faith looked at her body. Its attachment to her was fragile.

Is there anyone in it, she wondered.

She thought of moving her arm, and it moved obediently. She checked if all her senses were working. She could see the Master, yes. She could hear the faint sounds beyond the room, yes. She could smell the sweetness of Tierramedio. She touched her face and could feel its aliveness. There were other senses in her as well. They had entered her being and were waiting for an outlet.

It felt like all of Creation wanted to create through her, through anyone, through everyone.

"Go back to Borderfirma now," said the Master. "Remember, you are not your body, and you are not in your body. Your body is in Life. Use it until you need it no more, and then you will be happy to release it."

He smiled at Faith with the sort of smile that encompasses everything magnificent and everything tiny, seeing no difference between the two.

TWO HUNDRED LAUGHS

CHAPTER 14
BABYCAKES

I n *Wurt Wurt Koort:*

The end of summer was fast approaching. The shortening days signalled the need to enjoy what was left of bare feet, long grass, and bountiful sunshine. Bethany had been attending a course in the city over the last few weekends, so Faith and Aristotle had been coming to Wurt Wurt Koort to stay with Lentilly. At twelve and ten, respectively, Aristotle and Lentilly had great fun together as playmates.

Wurt Wurt Koort had an inexhaustible supply of natural adventure spots for children—the creek, the woods, and the town's old buildings. There was a children's park, but that fell short of the more interesting natural playgrounds and was only used as a last resort. Visits to Rybert's cafe were a daily highlight.

"Hello, cutenesses," said Rybert as Faith, Aristotle, and Lentilly entered the tearooms midmorning. "Let me guess what you want."

The children loved the guessing game. They all knew

Rybert wasn't guessing. He really could tell what they wanted. Even though this type of thing was baby play for Borderfirmarians, the children still enjoyed the game.

"Have I ever told you how I remember so many names?" Rybert asked the little group.

"No," chimed Lentilly and Aristotle together. "How?"

"By association," said Rybert.

"Lentilly is Lentil," he said, patting her head.

Lentilly was about to object as she had worked hard to get rid of her nickname.

Rybert interjected, "Sorry, bub. Once it's in my head, I can't get it out. I don't decide on the association. It just happens."

Turning to Aristotle, he said, "You look smart, so I think of Aristotle, the great Greek philosopher."

Aristotle was pleased and smirked at Lentilly, who responded with a whack to his arm.

"What about me?" asked Faith.

Rybert looked at her as if that was a ridiculous question.

"Anyone can see what you are made of, hun."

Faith smiled and said, "We are expecting a visitor today."

At that moment, Gabriel walked into the tearooms. Aristotle had been pestering Gabriel to come to Wurt Wurt Koort. He ran to Gabriel and jumped on him. Aristotle still possessed a childlike innocence. Teenage sophistication and aloofness had not even vaguely entered his mind. Faith wondered if he might skip the teenage attitude altogether. Lentilly also ran to Gabriel.

Until now, Gabriel had been polite but reserved with Aristotle's niece, sister, and brother. After all, they were new people to him. He could not remember the strong bond he had formed with them when he was in the

Borderfirma Mountains. Today, he was more relaxed and familiar.

Gabriel said hello to Faith and turned his attention to Rybert, who had been watching him the whole time. They eyed each other momentarily, and then looked away as if the other was of minimal interest. Underneath their easy, relaxed demeanours, neither was sure they wanted to share Faith and her family.

Both men belonged to the gay community and knew of each other, but had never met. Rybert rarely went to Darnall. However, some of the Boys of Darnall called to see him on their way to Waldmeer. Rybert would say the witches were enough for him without another group of bitches. He said that to the Boys themselves and to anyone else who would find it amusing.

"I can say that," he would laugh, "because I am one too."

People often replied, "What? A bitch or a witch?"

"Both," he would say with a wink.

"Did you know," said Rybert, deciding that a change of focus would be a good idea, "that young children laugh two hundred times a day and adults only laugh twenty?"

"Really?" said Faith.

"Yes, really," said Rybert, moving closer to Faith's face. "That's one hundred and eighty laughs gone. But where? Where do they go?"

Gabriel smiled with restrained amusement. He had to admit, Rybert was a character.

Turning to Gabriel, Rybert asked, "And what do they do when they get there, babycakes?"

"Okay, you two," said Faith, "The kids and I are going back to the cottage. I'll leave you to flirt."

"I'm not flirting," said Gabriel with mock annoyance.

Faith raised her eyebrows and headed for the door with the children. On the way out, she pondered that the tone of Gabriel's voice had a familiarity that she had not heard for a long time. She gave him a backward glance. Although he was attentively listening to Rybert, he was also watching her.

Something is different, thought Faith.

CHAPTER 15
FAITH-AMIRA

I ndeed, something *was* different. After twenty minutes, Gabriel appeared at the back door of Bethany's rented cottage.

"Come in," said Faith. "The children have gone to the creek, but shouldn't be too long."

"It's okay," said Gabriel.

Faith didn't know what was "okay", but Gabriel seemed to be gathering his thoughts, and she didn't want to interrupt him.

"I've been to see Erdo," said Gabriel.

He held his hands together. They didn't have their usual composure. He was sweating.

"Come and sit down. I'll get you a cup of tea," said Faith, even though he had just had coffee.

Gabriel put his arm on hers. He may have been unsteady, but his grip was still firm. Faith tried to be calm, but she felt a nervous energy in her body.

"I wanted to find out about Amira," said Gabriel, sitting on the lounge.

He looked piercingly at Faith. She wasn't sure what he would say, so she tried to show nothing on her face except acceptance of whatever was coming.

"I couldn't come to terms with her disappearance," he said. "I felt that she was alright. It wasn't worry. It was..."

"I couldn't accept that she was gone forever," he continued after a pause. "I was determined not to leave Erdo until he gave me a proper answer."

"What did he say?" asked Faith.

She was genuinely intrigued as to what Erdo would have come up with.

"He didn't say anything," said Gabriel.

"Oh," said Faith, somewhat disappointed.

"He didn't say anything," continued Gabriel, "because he wasn't there. I waited at the pond near the old walking bridge. After a while, I settled into listening to the creaking of the giant hardwoods. Two black swans were resting in the reeds. It was very peaceful. Then something strange happened. I'm not sure if I saw it in the water or my mind. It doesn't matter which because it's not the sort of thing you make up. I saw it all, Amira."

Amira? thought Faith.

"I saw the Borderfirma Mountains," said Gabriel. "I saw the children, Nina and Odin, and Indra and her snakes. I saw Aristotle and myself returning to Waldmeer through the frame."

The thought of the frame reminded Gabriel that it was the children's father, Zufar, who had given it to Aristotle. He frowned slightly but pulled himself back to the story.

"When I arrived back in Darnall, I couldn't cope with remembering Borderfirma, so Aristotle put a spell on me."

"It wasn't a spell," said Faith with a hint of motherly protectiveness.

"It was," said Gabriel. "You lot are full of spells. You put a spell on me. Maybe, you are a witch."

Faith laughed and then said quietly, "Love isn't a spell. Not if it's the sort of love that wakes us up. Then it's a spell-breaker, not a spell-maker."

Gabriel shrugged. He decided, years ago, that the best approach to Amira when she said things that went over his head was not to respond. He stood up and went to the window. He could see the creek and the children at the bottom of the hill.

"I saw your ten years in the Borderfirma Mountains," he said with a bit of sadness.

"Did it make you sad?" asked Faith.

"It was so much time away," said Gabriel.

He closed the back door, which had swung open in a sudden wind. They were silent for a few minutes. The breeze carried the children's voices up the hill and through the open window.

"The most important thing is that you know who I am," said Faith.

"That I do," said Gabriel.

Faith touched the middle of Gabriel's chest.

"I'm sorry that it was so long," she said. "I don't decide such things. Anyway, it wasn't long here. Only there."

Changing tone, Gabriel said, "I have to admit, I would prefer the younger version."

"I'm terribly sorry," said Faith with a smile.

"I'm going back to Darnall," said Gabriel. "Tell the children I'll see them in a few days."

He reached down, kissed her on the cheek, and left his face there for a moment.

"I'll see you too, Faith-Amira, in a few days."

That evening, Faith felt a great appreciation for the way things had worked out. She previously had no clue that Gabriel would, or could, realise that she was Amira. She wasn't sure, going forward, how he would assimilate that information into his mental concept of life. She reassured herself that what had been overwhelmingly confronting and confusing for him several months ago was no longer that. His mind must have been adjusting to a different reality without realising it.

There are bound to be problems, and life is not perfect, she thought, *but I can be grateful for all the pieces of life that are happy and harmonious. The other pieces will have their own way of falling into place. The less ego there is in both the good and the bad, the more the good things can grow, and the bad things will not be fed.*

She checked on the sleeping children, turned the lights off, lay on the bed, and closed her eyes.

PART II
MARRY AT ONCE

When the ocean comes to you as a lover,
marry, at once, quickly,
for God's sake.
Don't postpone it.
Existence has no better gift.

— RUMI

KEEP GOING

CHAPTER 16
MOVE

Michael, the shy sixteen-year-old boy Malik was training, stood in the cafe line. A group of similar-aged boys came in. Michael averted his eyes and hunched his shoulders as if he were trying to hide inside himself.

"Move back, idiot," said one of the boys. "We're ahead of you."

He was about to give his place to them when he noticed Malik sitting at a nearby table. Malik was watching intently. He didn't know what to do. If he didn't move, the boys would get angry. If he did move, he would have to face Malik at the next training session.

The boys also noticed Malik and paused to see if the gritty, no-nonsense man would do anything. All he did was return to his paper, so the boys returned to their former aggressive stance. Although the boys had turned their backs on Malik and could no longer see him, Michael could see him all too well.

Don't you fuckin' move, the Warlord's eyes said. *Stand up straight. Have I wasted myself on you? Have some self-respect.*

Michael looked away from Malik. He looked away from the boys. He stood there for a moment, gazing somewhere else entirely different, somewhere far away. In that faraway place, he caught an older, stronger glimpse of himself. It was calling to him. No, wait. Someone else was calling.

"Next," said the staff member for the third time.

"Me," said Michael. "It's me. I am next in line."

The boys did nothing. They returned to their dull, ridiculous conversation and looked like there had never been a problem. Malik stood up to leave. Michael caught the tail end of his expression—satisfaction. He wouldn't go so far as to think that the great Malik would be proud of someone like him, but he couldn't help smiling.

Michael's episode with the boys had been watched not only by Malik but also by another interested observer.

"Who's that big dude that just left?" said Rachael to Dayne.

Rachael had noticed Malik before the Michael incident happened. It was difficult not to notice him. His masculine face, well-built body, and confident posture made him very visible, especially to young women.

She was the talented weaver who worked in Handspun in Darnall. Her friend, Dayne, worked in its sister shop in Waldmeer. Not quite as wet behind the ears as when he started working in the bookshop, Dayne was nevertheless the same polite, hard-working, and humble person.

Last year, Amira suggested that Dayne help in the Darnall shop occasionally. She felt that Dayne and Rachael would be a good balance for each other and a good personal match. They were a good match and balance for each other, but they had not moved beyond friendship, even though Dayne pushed for it regularly.

Somewhat put out by Rachael's obvious and instantaneous interest in Malik, Dayne said offhandedly, "Oh, you know, that new guy at the Waldmeer Warriors. I don't know where he's from, but who cares? He's just a meathead."

Rachael looked at Dayne. It wasn't like him to disparage others, especially those he didn't know. Not wanting to bring up the topic again, she soon found another way to learn more about Malik. She went to the gym, requested a personal training session, and pointed to the photo of Malik on the wall when the owner asked who she wanted to book with.

He rolled his eyes and said insultingly, "You girls are all the same."

Although Rachael was no pushover, she decided to hold her tongue. Besides, it was partly true (but only partly). She was too smart to chase after someone for their looks alone. The main thing about Malik that caught her attention was his commanding presence. He had an unusual amount of self-assurance for someone his age. None of the boys in Waldmeer was like that.

Malik had already noticed Rachael in the cafe. He was pleased to see her booked in with him this morning. With the great interpersonal wisdom one has at twenty-four, he decided to be super tough on her in the training session.

Eventually, when exhaustion had worn away all the outer layers, Rachael blurted out, "You may be tough on the outside, but you are still a baby on the inside."

Malik looked shocked.

Realising that she had overstepped the mark, Rachael

said apologetically, "Oh, don't mind me. I'm delusional with tiredness."

However, the words had already been said and hung in the air with a stinging rawness. Malik wondered if he should get angry. He looked into Rachael's eyes for longer than was appropriate for a client. They were strong and kind eyes. He knew that combination. He knew it in his mother. He knew it in his sister, grandmother, and Nina. Even little Lentilly had some of it.

Then he did the only thing that one can do in such situations.

He fell in love.

CHAPTER 17
MINDSET

For the past few weeks, Gabriel drove to Waldmeer to visit Faith and her family on Wednesdays and Saturdays. Last night, only Faith, Gabriel, and Aristotle were in the house because Malik was at Rachael's. Gabriel decided to stay the night. He felt relaxed with Aristotle in the house because Aristotle viewed him as a pseudo-father. Malik, however, was a grown man and had prior rights. It seemed only fair to respect them.

In the morning, Faith woke before dawn. She hadn't slept well at all. She wanted to go for a walk because the fresh morning air would clear her mind. As it was still dark, she paced the house waiting for the first rays of light to reach the horizon. A tinge of red light crept over the water and into the edges of the vast, inky sky. Pulling on her cardigan, she closed the front door quietly and took the road down to the shops.

As she walked past the baker, she saw that the coffee machine was on.

"Can I be your first customer?" she smiled at the owner.

"It's always a pleasure to serve you, my dear, first or last," he replied.

Taking off her shoes on the beach, she could feel the soft, cool sand between her toes. The wind spiralled up and down the stretch of sand as if to have a final run before the day's people arrived to claim the beach.

She tried to sink into the problem that was bothering her. Even though she and Gabriel were pleased and relieved to be together again, all the same issues were still there. The only problem that had been resolved was that Gabriel now knew Faith was Amira. Also, he had some concept of the other realms, particularly the Borderfirma Mountains. No little achievement. However, other than that, he was his old self. Not that his old self was bad, but his old self conflicted with his newer, expanding self.

Feeling she needed to talk to someone, Faith thought of the Master from Tierramedio.

"Beautiful morning," said a male voice behind her.

She jumped as there had been no one on the beach as far as she could see. The Master seemed as comfortable as if he walked on the beach every morning.

"Gabriel is very changeable at this stage," he said. "His feeling for you does not change. That has remained constant because such things are not deliberate choices that one can decide to un-choose. What changes is the mindset from which he sees life."

A golden retriever came racing along the beach and bounded straight to the Master. He glanced down, rested a hand briefly on its head, and gestured lightly back towards the shore. The dog turned and ran off again, tail wagging wildly.

'When it is higher," continued the Master, "Gabriel is

confident in his attachment to you. When it is lower, he is pulled by the ego's offerings and by the people who share those values with him. He doesn't know that he is constantly gravitating between the two. Otherwise, it would be easy to fix, and it is not. One has to learn to recognise both mindsets and understand the consequences of each."

The Master looked at Faith with a twinkle in his eye and said, "He can't walk a straight line yet."

She laughed at the Master's joke.

They walked further, and he said, "We have designed an aid to help you learn to distinguish between the ego and the higher way. It is pain. The ego way inevitably leads to pain, even if it seems to satisfy temporarily. The higher way does not. It works. And it works harmoniously. It brings the sort of success that has no bitter aftertaste. It is not manipulative. It doesn't play one person against another. It doesn't feed anyone's fantasies. It is honest, and it protects the good."

The Master watched the seagulls as they searched for breakfast in the water. They were constantly perched on the edge of battle if one of them found something interesting.

"You are much more than the seagulls," he said.

"When Gabriel listens to his lower voice," said Faith, "it's not just that he can end up hurting me, but he can let other people hurt me who have been biting at the bit to do so. When Gabriel hurts me, at least I can reason with him that he is damaging the relationship, which, in his heart, he doesn't want to do. But if it's someone else, I have nothing."

The Master nodded and said, "Those who view you as detrimental to their causes will see you as an enemy. Whatever damage they think they can get away with, they will do. The more the ego wants something, the more vicious it can become. If it is not vicious immediately, it will simply be biding time."

He turned towards the cypress trees that lined the beach track. The Kookaburras loudly contributed their laugh to the cacophony of morning bird calls. The expression on his face became radiant.

"Everyone who comes to Earth has chosen the ego and must quickly or slowly learn its worthlessness and venom," he said.

Stepping back to indicate he was about to leave, the Master said, "Don't have a goal in mind when it comes to Gabriel. Your value is the love you share with the world. That love will always draw to you what you need. Remain faithful to the spirit you see in him and others, and you will save them a thousand years of tears."

When Faith returned home, Gabriel was dressed and ready to leave for Darnall. He looked as unsettled as she had felt earlier on.

"Keep going, love," she said as Gabriel kissed her goodbye and walked to the door to go to work. "You've done well to survive as long as you have. It gets easier."

TEARS AND SUNSHINE

CHAPTER 18
A THOUSAND
YEARS OF TEARS

F aith woke to someone's hand on her shoulder. She knew it wasn't Gabriel because he was in Darnall. Sitting upright, her eyes adjusted to the darkness.

"Thank God, it's you," said Faith as she recognised Zufar's silhouette.

Zufar looked at her calmly and waited for her to wake a little more.

"I have news," he said.

He wasn't smiling. Faith braced herself.

"We know life has no beginning and no ending," said Zufar.

Faith stopped listening.

No beginning and no ending, she repeated to herself. *That's a birth or a death.*

Her mother instinct kicked in. *Bethany, Malik, Aristotle, Lentilly?*

Sensing her panic, Zufar said, "They are all fine."

Someone has gone, thought Faith. *Who is missing? Who has gone?*

She sat upright and then said slowly, "It's my mother. She has gone, hasn't she?"

Zufar nodded. Faith's mother, known as Nanny, was eighty-five. Her five daughters each ruled a section of Borderfirma. Since Lady Faith's children had been born, Nanny lived in the Borderfirma Mountains because Faith was, in essence, a single mother, even though she was also a queen. Nanny had taken over the temporary running of the Borderfirma Mountains while Faith and her children were on Earth. Although firm, she was also caring. She was well-loved and respected and affectionately referred to as Queen-Mother Nanny by most Borderfirmarians.

Zufar told Lady Faith that it was not time for Malik or Bethany to leave Earth but that she must return to the Borderfirma Mountains immediately and take Aristotle with her.

Faith hesitated and looked towards Malik's room.

"I will wait until morning and explain to Malik what has happened," said Zufar.

Faith knew that Malik would be delighted to see his father. She then looked at the empty side of her bed where Gabriel sometimes lay.

Zufar, incapable of jealousy, said, "A thousand years of tears can only be voluntarily avoided. Go now."

CHAPTER 19
PLAYTIME IS OVER

In the Borderfirma Mountains:

Aristotle hung his legs from the top of the three-storey tree house in the palace gardens. He was glad to be back in Borderfirma, but it wasn't the same without Malik. Tree houses are meant for sharing—sharing adventures and secrets. He had only been away from Borderfirma for six Earth months, but many years had passed in the Borderfirma Mountains. Malik had long since outgrown the days of playing in trees.

Aware of Aristotle's need for company, Lady Faith looked at him over the dinner table and said, "I've asked Odin to visit. He'll be with us as soon as he can leave the Great Valley."

Aristotle's face brightened. He took solace in knowing Malik had lived and trained with Odin for ten years.

"I'm sure Odin could take you on some of his trips," said Lady Faith.

She knew that Aristotle was nothing like Malik and that a warrior was the last thing he was. However, Faith and Aristotle's departure from Earth and return to the Borderfirma Mountains had been sudden and unexpected. Aristotle needed something to distract him while he readjusted to palace life. After all, he was still a child, and Faith, herself, struggled to readjust.

CHAPTER 20
LOVE THAT'S REAL

I n *Wurt Wurt Koort:*

Rybert had one of his favourite playlists on in the Wurt Wurt Koort Tearooms. Timeless, catchy tunes that make you want to sing and dance, which is exactly what he was doing as he served the customers.

"This is an old song," said Lentilly when *Walking on Sunshine* began.

Grabbing Bethany by the hands, Rybert pulled her up to dance. He sang to her in his less-than-marvellous but more-than-enthusiastic voice about "buttercups" and "messing around" and "letting me down" and such things.

"Where's your mother?" asked Rybert. "I haven't seen her for a while."

Not yet having worked out an alibi, Bethany said, "She's in the mountains."

"Which mountains?" asked Rybert.

"The ones, ah... on the border," said Bethany unconvincingly.

Rybert looked confused.

"What's she doing there?" he asked.

"Err... looking after the family business," said Bethany.

"What business?" asked Rybert.

"Oh, um... lights," Bethany babbled. "We have a family business in making lights. You know, everyone needs light. The world needs lighting up."

Just shut up, Bethany told herself.

Dropping the subject, Rybert whispered into Bethany's ear, "Come back tonight at 7.00. My aunt is giving a talk to the witch coven, but you can come too."

"Your aunt?" asked Bethany.

"Yes, Aunt Charity," said Rybert with excitement. "She is the one who challenged the rogue head witch forty years ago, and then her daughter died, and she left Wurt Wurt Koort. She hasn't been back since, but they say she is now a powerful and accomplished witch."

That evening, Bethany and Lentilly sat at the edge of the small group and listened to Aunt Charity, who was around eighty-five. She didn't look powerful. She didn't even look like a witch. She did have unusually calm, deep, blue eyes and a very still body.

"As there are children with us tonight," said Aunt Charity, "we will finish the talk early and continue next week. All adults present have been chosen and are expected to return for future talks. It is not compulsory, but highly recommended that you take advantage of the opportunity."

"Witches!" shrugged Rybert.

He jumped up and said, "Time for something less serious."

He turned on his favourite playlist and started singing about "walking on sunshine" and "love that's really real".

CHAPTER 21
JUST GO

In Darnall:

After being in the Borderfirma Mountains for a week, Faith was told that she could return to Earth to see Gabriel for one hour. She materialised outside his apartment door. She assumed he would be pleased to see her. However, when he opened the door, once he recovered from the surprise, he wasn't pleased.

He stood there with that particular Gabriel look on his face, which said, *You hurt me. I'm angry. Don't talk to me. I want nothing to do with you. But don't go away. If you do, I'll be even madder.*

"Er... can I come in?" asked Faith.

Gabriel didn't say yes, but stepped aside.

Half an hour passed, with him virtually saying nothing. He busied himself with eating breakfast and getting ready for work. Eventually, Faith had to tell him that she only had an hour. She knew it would fan the fire, but the time was fast disappearing.

"Great," said Gabriel. "That's great. Why wait? Why don't you just go now?"

Oh dear, thought Faith.

Gabriel knew why Faith had to return to the Borderfirma Mountains because Malik had told him straight away.

He may not like it, thought Faith, *but I suppose one good thing is that Malik could tell Gabriel the truth about where I was. He didn't have to make something up.*

"I have responsibilities," said Faith.

"Responsibilities?" Gabriel glared. "To whom? Who exactly do you have responsibilities to?"

She had to admit he had a point.

Not wanting to watch her leave, Gabriel grabbed his jacket and said over his shoulder, "I'm going to work. Bye."

He didn't start work for another hour.

Faith sat in his apartment for ten more minutes, and then the pull to Borderfirma took her back to the palace.

HUSBAND

CHAPTER 22
ZEN DEN

In *Wurt Wurt Koort*:

"I need a bigger space for my Mystery School," said Aunt Charity as she showed Bethany the room she had set up in the back of Rybert's tearooms.

Bethany passed her hand over the bewitching glass ball, which had pride of place in the middle of the table.

How similar it looks to Nina's, she thought. *It has the same red velvet underneath and the same mysterious lights darting around inside.*

"It's one of a pair," said Aunt Charity. "The sister crystal ball went to a woman I met in a country shop sixty-five years ago. The shop was called *Zen Den.*"

Nina is Charity's age, thought Bethany.

"Where did the woman come from?" she asked.

"I don't know, said Charity. "She said it was somewhere quite difficult to get to. I assumed it was an inaccessible part of the country."

"Did you ever see her again?" asked Bethany.

"No," said Charity, "but over the years, she wrote to me

now and again. There's never a return address, but she always seems to find out my address. She wrote not long after my daughter died."

Her fingers moved absently over the edge of the crystal ball.

"It wasn't only the loss of a child," she said. "I lost everything at that time. As often happens after a child's death, I lost my marriage. I could no longer tolerate living here in Wurt Wurt Koort, so I lost my community. I did not know what anything meant anymore. I lost my confidence, my spiritual path, and ultimately myself."

Charity stood for a moment and moved a cup off the table, as if clearing space.

"After getting the letter, I decided to revisit the Zen Den. It was desperation. Desperation is the door of the Divine. I found a little book of love poems by the Persian mystic Rumi. The last thing I wanted was a book about love, as I had lost all the love in my life, but the book would not get out of my hand. It became my new companion."

Changing the topic, Charity said, "Rybert told me that your mother is back in the mountains running the family business."

"Yes," said Bethany with some shame. "The business is my responsibility. I've been trained for it for over ten years, but I will never be up to it. Anyway, when I was last in the mountains, a mystic told me that I would find my husband if I came to live here."

Looking around in all directions, she said, "There is no sign of him anywhere."

Both women laughed.

Charity opened Bethany's hand, put the worn book of love poems into it, and said, "A new friend for you."

CHAPTER 23
SNAKE IN THE GLASS

The little book of love poems seemed to have a power of its own. It insisted on remaining on the kitchen table. Not only did it want to be read, but it wanted to be read aloud.

In the morning, Bethany recited,

> Inside this new love, die.
> Do it now. Die,
> and be quiet. Quietness is the surest
> sign that you've died.
> Your old life was a frantic running
> from silence.

> — RUMI

In the afternoon, she read,

When the ocean comes to you as a lover,
marry, at once, quickly,
for God's sake.
Don't postpone it.
Existence has no better gift.

— RUMI

As she undressed for bed, Bethany chanted,

Love sits beside me like a private supply of
itself.
Our nakedness
together changes me completely.

— RUMI

A WEEK LATER, Bethany called into Charity's makeshift room in the cafe and said, "I have found a better place for your Mystery School."

"Where?" asked Aunt Charity.

"I have decided to return home to the mountains," said Bethany. "You can use the space I have created for my classes."

"What about your husband?" asked Charity.

"I have him," said Bethany, holding the Rumi book to her heart.

Bethany walked to the table and touched the ball.

"What is this?" she asked, pointing to a snake-like light on the outer ball.

She had seen the same light in Nina's ball.

"It's a snake," said Charity. "It lets me know the greatest point of danger for the person I am reading for."

"What is it pointing to?" asked Bethany.

"Oneself," said Aunt Charity. "It always points to the person themselves."

CHAPTER 24
MARRY THE OCEAN

I n the *Borderfirma Mountains*:

"You must be very proud of Bethany now that she is Queen of the Borderfirma Mountains," said Chester, Odin's ginger cat.

"Pride infers ownership," said Lady Faith. "You know I have no sense of ownership of my children."

Something in Lady Faith's voice sounded tense, so Chester talked carefully.

"Aristotle will be having a fine time with Odin," he said.

Chester had accompanied Odin from the Great Valley to the palace, but he had declined the month-long adventure into the other Borderfirma lands on the grounds of being "too old for such things".

"Malik will be glad to have you back in Waldmeer," said Chester, assuming that Lady Faith would return to Waldmeer as soon as possible.

"Malik is probably enjoying having the house to himself," said Faith.

"And Rachael too," said Chester with one slanty eye, presumably a wink.

Faith didn't laugh.

"Will you go to Darnall to be with Gabriel?" asked Chester.

"Gabriel is interested in someone else," said Faith flatly. "If he thinks I am putting energy into other relationships, he acts as if I have mortally wounded him. But he has little consideration for my feelings when it comes to what *he* does."

Faith picked up a perfect red autumn leaf from the mounting collection in the palace garden.

"It's not jealousy," she said. "If something is right for those we love, wouldn't we want them to take it?"

She threw the leaf into the shifting wind, kicked her way through a pile of leaves, and said, "Once, the Master told me, 'You can never lose someone you love, but relationships can get to the point where nothing else can be learned at that time.'"

As they walked back to the palace, Chester recited one of Bethany's love poems,

> When the ocean comes to you as a lover,
> marry, at once, quickly,
> for God's sake.
> Don't postpone it.
> Existence has no better gift.
>
> — RUMI

"Humans don't understand about marrying oceans," said Chester.

"No, they don't understand," said Faith, "but do I? Do I understand?"

WAY OUT

CHAPTER 25
DEATH ROW

An inter-dimensional trip to Tierramedio:

Faith had never before noticed the hallway beside the *Mirror of Life* in Tierramedio. It had a sign, *Death Row*. She certainly wouldn't have gone down the passage except that the Master appeared and pointed for her to do so. She accepted the invitation, knowing he would not lead her into danger. Not wholeheartedly, mind you.

She came to a room on her left. It looked like a hospital room. Entering, she saw a lone bed with a sleeping man. He was an older person, probably in the last stages of a fatal illness. She read the notice at the foot of the bed.

Age: 87
Name: Farkas

"Amira," said Farkas, opening his eyes, "you came."

"Of course, I came," said Faith.

Farkas had rarely been ill throughout his whole life.

"You're in pain, aren't you?" said Faith.

Farkas nodded.

"I'm going to get someone," said Faith. "Wait here."

"I don't think I'll be going anywhere," said Farkas.

At least, he still had his sense of humour.

She found a nurse at a desk and said unapologetically, "He's in pain. Fix it."

The nurse turned up the dial on the machine administering pain relief. Soon, Farkas relaxed.

"I'm not afraid of death," said Farkas, "but I am afraid of dying."

"You don't have to be afraid of either," said Faith.

She wanted to say that death was as much an illusion as this terrible hospital room, but its reality was overwhelmingly real to Farkas. She could tell he didn't want to be touched, so she sat a few feet away. Anyway, she felt that the less reality he gave to his body, the better he would feel.

"Thanks for being here," said Farkas. "Now that my life is over...."

"Please," said Faith, "try to see that nothing real is ever over."

Farkas listened more intently than he usually would have.

"As I was saying," he continued, "now that my life is over, I don't know why I had so much fear."

"Don't think about the past," said Faith. "You would like to get out of this room, wouldn't you?"

He stared at her as if he was considering whether she was speaking nonsense again or if she really knew a way out. The jury remained out on that one. The Master came to the door and beckoned Faith back into the hallway.

"This is only one possibility," said the Master, "a possible possibility. Everyone on Earth is on Death Row until they find a way out. It's not so hard to find the way out, but the problem is wanting to."

CHAPTER 26

A THOUSAND YEARS
OF HAPPINESS

In Tierramedio:

Faith heard a noise like a small party coming from further down the hallway. She entered a room on the right and looked around. It was the sort of communal lounge room one finds in an aged care facility. It was neat and clean and had a pleasant atmosphere. Nevertheless, it still had the feel of waiting death in the air.

She recognised a few people in the room as Gabriel's friends. After a while, they left, and only Faith and Gabriel remained.

"I didn't know you were here," said Gabriel, giving her a kiss.

While his visitors had been around, his expression had been bright and happy. Now that they were gone, he sat solemnly in a chair.

"I'm tired," he said.

He reached for a glass of water, drank some, and then carefully put it back on the table so as not to spill any with hands that were no longer young. He was probably in his nineties.

"You are still partying then?" said Faith.

Gabriel knew Faith all too well. He glared at her.

"I'm not a recluse," he said.

Turning towards a window with heavy, drawn curtains, he said, "Since I have been here, I've had a lot of thinking time."

He pulled himself up from the chair.

"I've spent too much of my life asleep," he said seriously.

"Yes?" said Faith hopefully.

"It's ridiculous," he said. "We spend a third of our life in bed."

"Oh," said Faith.

"I mean, I wouldn't mind if most of that time wasn't asleep," he added with a wink.

Faith didn't respond. She wanted this conversation to matter.

"And all the other times asleep?" she asked.

"What other times?" said Gabriel.

"Drinking, meaningless conversations, saying things you don't mean, not saying things you do," said Faith.

"Drinking isn't sleep," said Gabriel. "It's fun. You never quite got that. Fun!"

"Is it?" asked Faith.

He sat back into the chair with a bit of a thump.

"No," he said, "not really, but it's better than the alternative. I'm not you."

"Thank God for that," said Faith, "but do you want to hold onto empty things? We don't have to give anything up. They just need transforming. A thousand years of happiness would be much better than another thousand years of tears, don't you think?"

PART III
THE LAST USELESS BATTLE

FLOATING CAVE

CHAPTER 27
BORDERFIRMA BATTLE

In the Great Valley of the Borderfirma Mountains:

Nina passed her hand over the flickering crystal ball as Faith watched carefully. The last time Faith had seen the crystal ball was when Nina did a reading for Bethany and told her that she would visit Earth and find her future husband. With the help of Rybert's Aunt Charity, Bethany discovered her internal husband on Earth. It was the realisation of her spiritual completeness.

Bethany returned to take over the running of the Borderfirma Mountains with her newfound "husband" in tow. Since then, she had not been lacking attention from eligible men. It was time and destiny to see which of the wonderful young men was meant for her. Faith sometimes smiled to herself that it might not be one of the "wonderful" young men at all. It could be anyone, of any age, with any personality. She would leave that matter to Bethany, just as she had always listened to her own heart about such things.

Faith glanced at the row of religious statues overlooking today's reading. Krishna, with his flute, and Ganesh, with his elephant trunk, were at the head of the pack. Nina's expression became serious. She looked increasingly worried as she gazed at the lights reflecting the red velvet beneath. In semitrance, she said,

> The forces are gathering
> as we sit in this room.
> The darkness amasses
> bringing its doom.
>
> The sides are chosen,
> the wheels in motion.
> Go to the monastery,
> set your devotion.
>
> The last useless battle,
> someone will fall.
> Useless, but useful.
> For nothing, for All.

After discussion, Faith, Nina, and Odin decided the message meant that Evanora was preparing a Lowland's army to attack the other Borderfirma territories. The Borderfirma Mountains ran along the Lowland's border, so they were in imminent danger. Odin had had suspicions of a gathering force for some time.

"Which monastery is the crystal ball referring to?" asked Faith.

"The ancient monastery at the end of Indra and her father's property," said Nina. "Next to the sacred Floating Cave. In the absence of monks, Indra's father is the caretaker."

Although Indra's father, Peter, was known as the best snake catcher in the Lowlands, he was more than a simple snake catcher. He was all the things he seemed to be—honest, hardworking, practical, and generous—but he also came from the hidden line of Lowland mystics. They had been underground since the beginning of Evanora's rule and conscientiously worked towards ending her destructive and despotic reign.

CHAPTER 28
SALT AND SEX

One year later, in Waldmeer:

*O*ne year later, in Waldmeer:

Early one morning, Gabriel walked across the swing bridge to the Waldmeer Boathouse Cafe on the beach. As he sat drinking his coffee and staring at the waves, a man sat next to him. Gabriel thought he need not have sat so close as there were plenty of tables and they were the only customers. Nevertheless, he couldn't help feeling drawn to the stranger. There was something trustworthy about him.

The stranger said casually, "I believe you are Faith's friend?"

"Yes," said Gabriel in surprise.

Not offering his name, how he knew Faith, or how he knew Gabriel, the stranger continued, "I saw her just then in Cypress Lane. If you hurry down, I'm sure she will still be there."

Unbeknown to Gabriel, the stranger was the Master of Tierramedio. Leaving his coffee, Gabriel headed for Cypress

Lane. He hadn't seen Faith for a year. It was a long time. As he strode through the tunnel of trees, his thoughts became still and peaceful. He felt that his body was disappearing. It wasn't an unpleasant feeling, so he didn't stop it. Next thing he knew, he was in the Borderfirma Lowlands.

AT FLOATING CAVE, in the Borderfirma Lowlands:

Floating Cave was sacred and secret. It wasn't particularly hidden, but only those meant to find it did so. It was a single cave within a large rock formation at the far end of Indra and her father, Peter's, property in the Lowlands.

An underground spring fed into the peaceful rock sanctuary, creating a lukewarm pool. There was no natural outlet for the water to pass through the cave, so the water gradually evaporated, leaving large reservoirs of salt and other minerals.

Salt ponds are highly buoyant. It is impossible to sink in them, and you have to make a concerted effort to roll over. Not that you would, as you would probably get salt in your eyes.

Unlike some salt lakes and ponds, Floating Cave did not smell. Nor was it infested with brine shrimp and flies, which make some salt lakes unpleasant to swim in. Part of the Floating Cave's mystery was how the water remained so clear, clean, and fresh-smelling. It was as pristine as a commercial flotation tank, but it was much more beautiful and healing.

Peter told Faith that he believed the monks, who had lived for centuries in Floating Cave Monastery, extracted chlorine from the surrounding plants and treated the water. That sounded the most plausible explanation, except for one thing. Since Evanora had ruled the Borderfirma Lowlands, the monks had disappeared, leaving none in the monastery. Still, the water remained pure.

Faith stood at the entrance of Floating Cave. Gabriel stood behind her.

A year had passed both in Borderfirma and Waldmeer. This was the first time they had seen each other in that time. They hadn't spoken yet.

Gabriel appeared next to the ancient bell of the Floating Cave Monastery minutes ago. The bell was a portal for inter-dimensional travel. It announced visitors with a ring and forewarned their departure with another.

Walking a few metres into the cave and gladly away from the early winter wind, Faith stood facing the quiet pond. Without glancing back, she began to undress—cardigan, shirt, shoes and socks, long skirt, underwear.

She stood naked before the mystical water. Her white skin reflected some of the little light at the opening end of the cave.

Gabriel had not yet entered the cave, but his gaze had not left her silhouette. As she walked slowly into the pool and began to fade from sight, he instinctively entered. His eyes adjusted to the cave interior, and he saw Faith beckoning him into the water.

Once undressed, Gabriel walked into the water, lay back in the dense, consuming liquid, and effortlessly floated. The water held his head like a pillow. It was body temperature and very comfortable.

Amazing, he thought.

Faith reached for his hand and gently pulled him towards her. She slowly manoeuvred them both towards the far end of the cave.

It was very dark. Gabriel held onto her hand firmly.

She put his hand on the cave wall so that he could feel its reassuring stability. She then slowly moved around the cave so that Gabriel knew how big the pool was.

He lightly touched the wall as Faith pushed them around the perimeter. His fingers ran over the particles of salt that were at the waterline.

Then Faith put her hand on Gabriel's chest and stroked it rhythmically to get him to relax more deeply. *Relax, relax. Everything is fine. You are safe.*

Gabriel could hear a low, continuous rumbling sound. It seemed to be coming from deep in the ground, or maybe it was the reverberation of noise from the rocks above. It wasn't disturbing. It was soothing, like a mysterious mantra one repeats without ever learning what the words mean.

Moving her hand from Gabriel's chest, Faith rested it on his stomach. She lightly pushed her feet into the cave wall and sent them sailing back to the entrance.

With a little more light, Gabriel felt increasingly confident.

Again, Faith gently pushed her feet into the cave wall and sent them gliding back to the darker, deeper end of the cave.

Gabriel enjoyed the serene movement through the water. He stretched his body in all directions. He felt that he was in the land's womb. The tension was leaving his muscles as the saltwater dragged it into the bowels of that same land.

Slowly, almost imperceptibly, Faith drew her hand from

Gabriel's stomach to his lower abdomen. The feeling of relaxation, which had settled at a pleasant plateau, now went in the other direction.

He could feel a growing pressure within himself. Passion. That feeling, he knew. His body was tensing again, not with stress but with desire.

He drew Faith closer to him, and, to his surprise, even with their weights combined, they still didn't sink. He ran his hand down her back and onto her outer thigh. Faith responded by quickening her breath.

Soon, both of their breaths were intensely reverberating around the cave.

Then, after a while, all was quiet again.

Empty, full, timeless.

Although they had released each other, Faith kept her fingers lightly on his arm as they lay motionless in the supportive water.

Gabriel no longer wanted to move, stretch, or do anything with his body. He temporarily felt that he didn't even have a body in that altered sensory environment of the cave. Everything had such a perfect equilibrium that it was difficult to differentiate one thing from another, one body from another, one being from another.

Later—it may have been two hours or five minutes (it was hard to tell)—Faith pushed her feet, one last time, into the back wall, and they floated towards the entrance.

Exiting the water felt like dragging a second body as they regained their weight. The air was biting against their wet, naked skin, so they quickly dressed.

The ancient bell of Floating Cave Monastery was ringing, which meant it was time for Gabriel to return to Waldmeer.

He touched the bell, smiled, and said as he disappeared, "Maybe, next time, we won't use the cave. It's very relaxing, but the salt water is a bit stinging."

Faith turned her face to the soft sun as Gabriel faded from sight and thought with amusement, *I didn't hear any complaints when we were in the cave.*

GATHERING THE FORCES

CHAPTER 29
FIRST WARRIOR

At *Floating Cave Monastery, in the Borderfirma Lowlands:*

Since Nina's reading a year ago, Faith had been living alone at Floating Cave Monastery. She often visited Nina and Odin in the Great Valley, as Aristotle was living with them.

Sometimes Aristotle came to the Lowlands to be with his mother. He stayed in Indra and Peter's cottage, as Faith felt that the vibration of the monastery was too intense for Aristotle's delicate spiritual constitution. Aristotle and Indra were now thirteen years old, no longer children, but a long way off adulthood.

As the monastery had been abandoned decades ago, Faith spent most of her time fixing it. When she first arrived, it was early winter, and the building was freezing. Her most urgent mission was to get the heating working. Most days, Peter ambled across to the monastery to help Faith with all the practical things that he was so good at, including getting rid of snakes in the building.

It didn't take long for the centuries of spiritual practices and prayer, which had been the lifeblood of the place, to refill the corridors and crevices of the building. It seemed to Faith that it was re-forming a protective, healing energy field within and around the building.

After fixing the heating and her bedroom, Faith cleaned and prepared the monk's rooms. She was told that they should be made ready for the gathering forces. Each room had two single beds, as the monks shared a room with a fellow monk. She was also told that when the forces started to arrive (which was imminent), the rooms should be filled in order of those who appeared.

Faith turned off the lights in Floating Cave Monastery, except for the upstairs hallway and her small bedroom. It was only nine o'clock, but she was used to going to bed early and waking before first light. As she was about to retire, the ancient bell rang.

"What?" she said. "Someone is coming now?"

Who will be my first warrior? she wondered as she descended the stairs and headed for the peeling, green entrance door at the opposite end of the hallway.

"Rybert?" she said in surprise. "What are you doing here?"

How does Rybert know about the Borderfirma Battle? she thought.

Anyway, he wasn't exactly the warrior she was expecting.

"That's not very nice," said Rybert, "after all my effort to get here. You could say, 'Thank you for coming.'"

"Yes, of course, thank you," said Faith. "But how did you get here, and why are you...?"

She stopped mid-sentence and reminded herself that she

was not in control of who was coming and why. Besides, she was pleased to see him.

"Wait till I get my dressing gown, and we'll have some tea. The kitchen is second on the left."

Faith turned on the lights again and hurried upstairs to get something warm to wear. Over tea and toast, Rybert explained that his Aunt Charity told him that she had seen the gathering of two armies in her crystal ball, but she didn't recognise the landscape or most of the faces.

"She reluctantly told me that the ball said I must travel to the battle," said Rybert. "I told her I am no soldier, but she said that the ball doesn't make mistakes. She didn't want to tell me about it. I suppose she was worried."

After a pause, Rybert added rather sweetly, "Is it okay that I have come?"

"It's not my decision who comes," said Faith. "Who comes, comes."

That wasn't the answer Rybert wanted. Faith looked at him more closely. Always, he had been the friend of all, the comedian, the life of the party. Now, he was being something else. She reconsidered her response. On many levels, he had taken a great risk to be here. He deserved a better answer than what she had given him.

"Thank you for coming," said Faith with her hand on her heart.

She showed him his room, turned off the lights for the second time, and headed to her bedroom upstairs.

Climbing into bed, she thought with half-amusement and half-concern, *If Rybert is my first warrior, it's going to be a very weird battle.*

CHAPTER 30
RIDICULOUS

I n *Waldmeer:*

Gabriel's recent visit to Floating Cave seemed to have an after-effect on his state of mind. He couldn't settle to anything. He was sluggish and disconnected. He went to cafes, but decided he wasn't hungry. He picked up his phone, but decided he was not interested in talking to anyone. He had to concentrate to get through his teaching classes. Floating Cave and Faith were constantly in his thoughts.

On a clear, starry evening, a week after his last adventure, he returned to Cypress Lane and cautiously proceeded through the tunnel of dark trees.

～

In the Borderfirma Lowlands:

The evening after Rybert arrived at Floating Cave Monastery, the ancient monastery bell rang again as Faith prepared for bed.

I don't know why it can't bring my warriors first thing in the morning, thought Faith, *rather than last thing at night when I am tired.*

She opened the green monastery door, and there stood Gabriel. Faith was becoming increasingly concerned about who she was being sent. Not only were they dreadful warriors, but, more concerning, the time was fast approaching when the Borderfirma Lowlands would be a dangerous place to be. She had already told Aristotle to return to the Great Valley and not come back to the Lowlands until after the battle.

"Come in, Gabriel," said Faith rather distractedly. "You have to share a room with Rybert."

Gabriel went to object, but Faith put up her hand.

"I don't decide," she said. "In order of arrival, the rooms are to be filled."

Gabriel and Rybert looked at each other in the small monk's room.

Turning his back on Rybert, Gabriel said quietly to Faith, "I'm *not* sharing a room. Unless it's with you. Can't I sleep in your room?"

"It's a monastery," said Faith. "No sex in monasteries."

"I don't just think about sex, you know," said Gabriel indignantly.

"Calm the farm," said Rybert, who decided to join the conversation.

"You have me, pumpkin," he said to Gabriel with a wink.

Gabriel groaned and sat with a thump on the bed.

"Ah, that's my bed," said Rybert, "unless you want to share."

Gabriel pushed past Rybert and went to the other bed, but he couldn't help smiling a little. Rybert was a funny guy.

"Just don't touch me," said Gabriel.

"Don't worry," Rybert said, being his more assertive self. "I have no intention of touching you, Princess."

Faith looked at them, shook her head, and walked to her own bedroom.

Ridiculous, she thought as she ascended the stairs. *They are both ridiculous. Ridiculous together. And the world's most ridiculous warriors. Tomorrow they both have to go home.*

CHAPTER 31
COMING AND GOING

Faith and Rybert walked to the top of a nearby hill at sunrise. This part of the Lowlands was mostly grassland. The wind was cold and unfriendly, and there were hardly any trees to minimise its sweep across the hillside. They pulled their coats tighter. The sun would warm the land a little later, but its warmth was only a promise at the moment.

"I don't want to go back to Wurt Wurt Koort," said Rybert. "I wouldn't have come if I weren't intending to stay."

"Yes," said Faith, "I understand that."

She looked out over the land. Soon, the entire hillside and beyond would be filled with the armies from the Borderfirma territories. Her sisters—Pearl, Melba, and Rose—had sent armed forces. Bethany had also sent the Borderfirma Mountain's defence force under Odin's command. The armies of all the Borderfirma territories were usually dormant. This was a rare and unhappy occasion.

Before Evanora's rule, the Lowlands was a well-functioning and harmonious place. One would think the

Lowlands people would have refused to obey Evanora. However, Evanora was no fool and knew how to groom the psyche of people who were generally less clever, determined, and energetic than she.

Sensing that she was not making any progress in convincing Rybert to go home, Faith said, "When we give our attention and love to anything in life, it is a significant offering. We only have so much time. What we spend it on and who we give it to will determine the course of our life, and I am very grateful that you came. Nevertheless, I must ask you to return home. If you don't want to go back to Wurt Wurt Koort, then go somewhere else, but you have to return to Earth."

Faith could see by Rybert's defeated expression that he would go, but he looked hurt. His hurt was her hurt, too.

"Don't be sad," said Faith. "You can't be harmed for something you have done that is good."

Rybert looked unconvinced.

"You will see," she said. "Life doesn't punish us for being true. Let's go back to the Monastery now. Gabriel also needs to return to Earth. He will go with you as he is used to coming and going."

NOT ON MY WATCH

CHAPTER 32
US AND THEM

I n the *Borderfirma Lowlands:*
     Every day, for the week since Gabriel and Rybert left, more and more soldiers arrived from the Borderfirma territories. They camped on the monastery hill and numerous other hills beyond. As the thousands came, so was the Borderfirma Lowlands army amassing on the opposite side of the land. Impending doom hung heavily beneath the sky, which, regardless, remained a cheery blue with cloud puffs skipping along a carefree path.

Odin kept repeating a phrase dear to his heart, "Not on my watch." Faith knew he was reaffirming his commitment to protect her, her family, the Borderfirma Mountains, and all he considered worth fighting for. He was usually a force to be reckoned with, but with the added fire of danger, his intensity was not to be underestimated.

Faith had her version of *not on my watch* running through her mind. *Not on my watch—I am responsible for these people's lives. Not on my watch—no one must be lost.*

Her version included the Lowlands, its army, and even

Evanora. Unlike Odin, who still perceived life as *us and them,* Faith had no perception of *us and them.* To her, the Lowlands army was as important as her own. The problem was obvious and nasty. Under Evanora's rule, the Lowlands army not only perceived an *us and them,* but they were deadly intent on destroying the *them.*

Further, with every soldier arriving at the monastery hills, the intent of the Lowlands force grew greater from fear and propaganda. Although the Lowlands people were initially reluctant to join Evanora's army, they now flocked to it under the notion of self-defence.

Faith did not know what to do. Her first problem was how to keep everyone safe. Her second was that the conflict was escalating at an alarming rate. She did not know the answer, but it was her responsibility to find it and find it fast.

She went to Floating Cave, looking for the answer. The quiet, dark, wet air was calming. Sitting motionless at the edge of the salt pool, she asked, *How can this conflict be resolved without doing damage?*

She listened.

And listened more.

If the answer was there, she couldn't hear it.

All she heard was, *No one must be lost.*

That seemed impossible.

CHAPTER 33
DREAM

As she was going to sleep in her monastery bed, Faith heard the muffled, distant sounds of men around campfires. Some hours later, she had a lucid dream.

She was, not surprisingly, in a type of battle. At one critical point, she decided that she must venture on alone. Knowing that her friends would be unwilling to return to safety without her, Faith told them they must take the children to safety and that she would return soon. She also told them she would use the magic golden armour she possessed. While wearing it, she could not be hurt. Reluctantly, her friends agreed and let her go on alone.

When she arrived at the edge of the space where she would face the enemy, she felt the armour was terribly heavy and cumbersome. She didn't want to wear it, but would be completely vulnerable without it. A group of little birds arrived. They were very similar to the sweet ones that always accompanied Mullum-Mullum. They told her that wearing the magic protective armour would do more harm than good.

"Take it off, take it off," the little birds repeated.

Faith was reluctant to take off the armour as she would be instantly killed by the ferocious enemy as soon as she entered the arena. Nevertheless, something about the little birds was so pure and trustworthy. Besides, they seemed to be speaking for an ancient voice that wanted to be remembered.

Irresistibly, the voice drew her deeper into its being, and she, for better or worse, took off the armour and stepped into the arena. She was afraid, yes. She thought she would be killed, but her trust in the little birds and their invisible Master was so great that she decided to do it anyway.

A strange thing happened as she walked into the sweltering heat of the arena, ready to face her fate. She did not burn under the enemy's fire. Her body disintegrated, not because it was being destroyed but because it was no longer there. Yet her essence was totally present and conscious in the arena. As she had no body, she could not be hurt or touched.

The enemy passed through her and, perceiving no threat, went on its way.

CHAPTER 34
FIRE-EYES

The following morning, Lady Faith slowly and deliberately dressed. She went to the hillside and called Odin and the three other Borderfirma commanders. She had a low fire burning in her eyes. It made her look different, stronger, but also less reachable.

Odin looked at her several times to understand why she looked like that and what she was doing.

"I have called you to me," said Lady Faith, "as it is time for you to take your armies back to your territories. We will not be fighting the Lowlands army. As for me, I will be staying here."

Predictably, Odin and the other commanders were shocked and highly reluctant to accept her command.

"Lady Faith," said Odin, "the Lowlands army will certainly attack, and if you remain here, they will, without doubt, kill you. I cannot allow...."

It was seldom necessary to use the full force of the fire inside Faith, but when it came, it came without apology. It came from Beyond. When present, Faith had no personal identity. Having no identity and therefore nothing to lose, the force was given free rein. Therein lay its power.

"It is not a request," said Lady Faith with steely resolve.

She stared at Odin until, realising it was useless to resist, he conceded. The three other commanders likewise lowered their eyes and headed for their relevant army groupings.

Lady Faith turned to go but stopped and called after them, "Wait. There is one more thing."

Odin and the commanders looked at Lady Faith with tense, worried faces. The fire in Lady Faith's eyes was already subsiding.

"You need not worry," she said more softly. "I will not be here alone. Each of you must send me your best mystic."

The commanders now looked confused as well as worried.

"Only one mystic," smiled Lady Faith reassuringly, "but your best one, please."

CHAPTER 35
INNOCENCE

By the end of that week, the mystics started to arrive at Floating Cave Monastery.

Lady Pearl was delighted to have found one of the original Floating Cave Monastery monks who had fled to her land when Evanora took control of the Lowlands. He was elderly but had lost none of his devotion or ability.

Lady Melba sent her most respected religious leader.

Lady Rose sent a local farmer known amongst the people as a healer. He never took money for healing but was brutally honest to anyone who knocked on his cottage door with a questionable mentality or ethics.

There was still no one from Faith's land, the Borderfirma Mountains. Bethany was having trouble deciding who their best mystic was. She sent a message to Nina in the Great Valley to ask her crystal ball. Although Bethany did not find out who the ball had chosen, she received a message that Odin would accompany the mystic to the Lowlands and remain with him as protector.

Odin and his charge reached the border of Borderfirma

and the Lowlands. They had passed the exit sign, which read,

Thank you for visiting us.
If you must dream a dream,
at least make it a happy one.

In the distance, Odin could see the Lowlands entry sign. It had an image of two snakes attacking each other. A king cobra was biting a python, and the python was constricting the king cobra. Odin chatted brightly to his charge to counteract the negative vibe of the sign. It was probably more for his own benefit. His charge didn't seem bothered by the sign at all.

When Lady Faith opened the green monastery door, her face fell. It was Aristotle.

Not my child, she thought. *It's too dangerous.*

She then corrected herself and thought, *Everyone is my child, and no one is in danger.*

"The crystal ball said that Aristotle's innocence will protect him," Odin whispered to Lady Faith.

Nevertheless, Odin looked like he was there for backup, just in case the ball didn't know what it was talking about. And that is how Odin and Aristotle ended up sharing one of the monk rooms in the monastery.

Faith could hear their laughter as she walked along the hall. It made her smile. The tension was breaking up. Was that foolish? Would it help? Would it make for a sad closing curtain or a solution?

FOR NOTHING, FOR ALL

CHAPTER 36
ANNIHILATION

Although the Lowlands army was primed and ready to attack, the little group at Floating Cave Monastery did nothing—nothing out of the ordinary, that is.

The six household members (Faith, Aristotle, Odin, and the three mystics from the other Borderfirma lands) went about their day as calmly and quietly as if it were peacetime. It's not that they sat in meditation all day. They had their regular prayer and meditation times, typical of any monastery.

However, they also gardened, cooked, and cleaned. They went shopping in the local village. They talked about minor things with the villagers and asked about their lives. They volunteered at numerous local charities. They did normal things, but they did them with abnormal love and inclusiveness.

The Lowlands folk near Floating Cave Monastery started to relax and forget about the conflict. They went about their business and stopped talking about the coming war.

Their attitude gradually spread to the rest of the Lowlands so that, over a few months, the steam went out of the battle, and most of Evanora's soldiers decided to return to their homes and former jobs.

Of course, Evanora tried to stop them. However, her hateful, fear-provoking speeches didn't have the same effect as they did previously. As each soldier left, Evanora's state of mind deteriorated until she became quite mad. Her commanders decided to commit her to a psychiatric hospital.

Evanora had lost her power. If no one listened to her, she could do no harm. The spell had been broken without drama, without fanfare. The people lost faith in their leader. They lost interest in what she was doing and saying.

To an ego such as Evanora, that was a fate worse than death. To be ignored is equivalent to annihilation. To not exist is any ego's greatest fear.

CHAPTER 37
NO ACCIDENT

"**A**ristotle and Indra are quite the quintessential soul mates, aren't they?" commented Faith to Odin one morning.

She watched Indra feeding her snakes and Aristotle standing a safe distance away with dead mice. Aristotle didn't enjoy it, but he wanted to be with Indra. He always wanted to be with Indra.

"There is one more thing that Nina's crystal ball said about Aristotle other than him being the Borderfirma Mountain's best mystic," said Odin.

He took a breath as if he was still processing the information.

"What is it?" asked Faith, eager to know.

"It said that Aristotle and Indra will marry at twenty and jointly take over the leadership of the Borderfirma Lowlands," said Odin.

"Really?" said Faith.

She sat down to think about the implications of what Odin had said.

"They don't know that, do they?" asked Faith.

"No," said Odin.

"Good," said Faith. "They have seven years."

She remembered that Aristotle and Indra shared the same birthdate.

I suppose it is no accident that they came here together, she thought. *One was born in a palace, and one in the simple home of a snake catcher, but they were surely going to find each other.*

That evening, Faith said, "I will stay here until Aristotle and Indra no longer need me."

"I will, too," said Odin.

A few days later, Odin said, "A strange thing has happened. This morning, I passed the Lowlands entry sign. It no longer has two snakes killing each other. There are still two snakes on the sign, but they are intertwined in a figure eight."

"Neither is poisoning or suffocating the other," said Faith.

CHAPTER 38
IN HIS HEART

I n *Waldmeer:*

A few months had passed in Waldmeer. Winter had had its run, and it was now early spring.

Gabriel was enjoying his drive to Waldmeer from Darnall. He looked at everything with fresh eyes. Perhaps, he was looking as one does when it will be the last time one sees something very familiar. Anyway, the countryside was beyond beautiful.

He parked next to Cypress Lane and walked along the main beach. The tide was low. The sea was relatively calm. The sky was a mix of silver and grey clouds. The morning sun shone at an angle that turned everything into a mirror. It was difficult to distinguish where the sand, sea, sky, and clouds started and ended. All merged into one brilliant shimmer of light.

He stopped for a coffee at the Waldmeer Boathouse Cafe and looked around for the stranger he had met there last time. He felt sure he would come. He waited and thought about the last few months. He had tried to settle back into work and normal life, but he was irreversibly changed. Besides, life wasn't the same without Faith-Amira. He knew in his heart that, this time, she wasn't coming back.

CHAPTER 39
NOT HERE

One week later, in Waldmeer:

Malik couldn't get Gabriel out of his mind. That afternoon, he decided to visit him when he was in Darnall. He called into the Darnall College because he assumed Gabriel would be at work.

"Not here," said the receptionist when Malik asked to see Gabriel.

"What do you mean?" asked Malik.

"He left last week. Doesn't work here anymore," said the receptionist.

"Oh," said a surprised Malik. "Thanks."

Malik then drove to Gabriel's apartment and was equally surprised when another man opened the door.

"Not here," said the man. "We live here now. Moved in last week. Don't know him. Don't know where he is."

Seeing that the guy was anxious to get on with his day, Malik said, "Thanks," and left.

In bed that evening, Malik said to Rachael, "Gabriel has gone."

"Where?" asked Rachael.

"I don't know," answered Malik. After a few minutes, he said, "I think he has gone to be with Mum."

Rachael nodded. She knew enough about Malik's family not to probe too deeply into their comings and goings.

She touched his arm and said, "You have me. We have each other."

Malik smiled at her.

"And a beautiful house," added Rachael happily.

Malik smiled again and rolled over to go to sleep. His days were full, and he was tired. He had much to do in this world.

CHAPTER 40
THE LAST USELESS BATTLE

O*ne week ago, in Waldmeer:*
On that day, at the Waldmeer Boathouse Cafe, the stranger did come to Gabriel as he had anticipated. He didn't say anything but beckoned Gabriel into Cypress Lane. They walked peacefully together through the flickering light.

Gabriel felt that there were many questions he should ask and many worries that he should explain, but, in the end, he didn't say any of them. He simply listened. It was a good choice.

The Master repeated Nina's poem from the crystal ball.

The last useless battle;
someone will fall.
Useless but useful,
for nothing, for All.

"The one that falls is our small self," said the Master. "Indeed, it must fall."

He looked through the trees to the beach. The light was bouncing between sea, sand, and sky. Its frequency seemed to heighten with the Master's gaze.

"Every battle is useless," said the Master, "because, ultimately, they are not necessary. Nevertheless, every battle is important because we cannot win a battle we don't know we should be fighting. It is all for nothing and also all for everything. Do you understand?"

Gabriel said honestly, "No, not really."

After a moment, he added with a combination of resignation and determination, "But I'm going, anyway."

"Good enough," said the Master as Gabriel strode along Cypress Lane and faded from view.

The End

SUMMARY OF
WALDMEER SERIES

A multi-generational journey of spiritual awakening, healing, and the spaces between worlds.

Beneath the surface of an idyllic coastal village, unseen forces stir. Waldmeer is a place where the visible and invisible meet—where inter-dimensional realms brush against everyday life, and where emotional truths rise quietly but undeniably.

Told across seven books, the *Waldmeer Series* follows Maria–Amira from the groundedness of her rural home to the doorways into higher realms of perception and spiritual transformation. Around her, those she loves and seeks to help are drawn into their own awakenings, resistances, and reckonings.

Waldmeer moves between ordinary moments and otherworldly initiations. Between earthly love and higher love. Between who we think we are... and what we truly are.

At times tender, at times confronting, these stories unfold in layers—personal, relational, and metaphysical.

ABOUT THE AUTHOR

On the beach at Lorne, Australia (the coastal village Waldmeer is based on).

Donna Goddard is a spiritual author whose work blends clarity, devotion, and metaphysical insight. With more than twenty published books across spiritual nonfiction, fiction, poetry, and children's literature, she writes to uplift consciousness and offer healing through words.

Donna's Facebook author page has over 400,000 followers worldwide, and her YouTube channel has received 4 million views. Her books are read by spiritual seekers globally and are known for their honesty, poetic style, and transformative energy.

Her writing is an offering—to help others awaken their own inner spirit, trust its guidance, and create a life of depth, beauty, and quiet joy.

All links at https://linktr.ee/donnagoddard

Ratings and Reviews

Donna would be grateful for any ratings or reviews.

ALSO BY DONNA GODDARD

Fiction

Waldmeer Series: A Spiritual Fiction Series
Nanima Series: Spiritual Fiction
Enanika Series: Visionary Fiction
Riverland Series (children's fiction 6 to 9 years)
Foxie (children's fiction 7 to 12 years)

Nonfiction

Love and Devotion Series
Sweet Spirit Series
Consciousness Series
Meditation Series
Poetry Series
Love's Longing
Dance: A Spiritual Affair
Writing: A Spiritual Voice